Angelina Ballerina™

Best Big Sister Ever!

By Katharine Holabird
Based on the illustrations by Helen Craig

Simon Spotlight

New York   London   Toronto   Sydney   New Delhi

To my beloved grandchildren, Max, Charlie, Milo, and Isabella —K.H.

This book is a work of fiction. Any references to historical events, real people, or real places are used fictitiously. Other names, characters, places, and events are products of the author's imagination, and any resemblance to actual events or places or persons, living or dead, is entirely coincidental.

SIMON SPOTLIGHT
An imprint of Simon & Schuster Children's Publishing Division
1230 Avenue of the Americas, New York, New York 10020
This Simon Spotlight edition May 2023
© 2023 Helen Craig Ltd. and Katharine Holabird.
The Angelina Ballerina name and character and the dancing Angelina logo are trademarks of HIT Entertainment Limited, Katharine Holabird, and Helen Craig.
Cover and interior illustrations by Mike Deas
All rights reserved, including the right of reproduction in whole or in part in any form.
SIMON SPOTLIGHT and colophon are registered trademarks of Simon & Schuster, Inc.
For information about special discounts for bulk purchases, please contact Simon & Schuster Special Sales at 1-866-506-1949 or business@simonandschuster.com.
Book designed by Claire Torres
The illustrations for this book were rendered in pen and watercolor.
The text of this book was set in Bembo.
Manufactured in the United States of America 0323 OFF
10 9 8 7 6 5 4 3 2 1
ISBN 978-1-6659-3594-4 (hc)
ISBN 978-1-6659-3593-7 (pbk)
ISBN 978-1-6659-3595-1 (ebook)

Contents

Chapter One

Blueberry Pancakes for Breakfast

It was a golden autumn morning in the village of Chipping Cheddar, the kind of day that made Angelina feel like dancing everywhere. As soon as she woke up, Angelina leapt out of bed and practiced pirouettes around her bedroom in her nightgown, humming her favorite ballet music to herself.

Angelina was excited because today was a special day—the very first day of another year at Chipping Cheddar Elementary! Angelina couldn't wait to see all her friends and meet her new teacher. The night before, she had carefully packed her school notebooks and pencils in her backpack, so everything was ready. She didn't want to be late today!

Angelina quickly brushed her teeth, put on her favorite pink dress, and tied a pink bow in her hair. She found her new school backpack where she'd left it near her bed. She wanted to surprise her parents by being ready early.

"Ta-da!" Angelina announced. "Here
I am, all dressed for school!"

Angelina's father looked in at her with a smile. "Well done, Angelina," Mr. Mouseling said. "Have you seen your little sister? Today is a special day for her too."

Angelina's little sister Polly was going to her first day of preschool today, and Angelina knew she'd need help getting ready. "Angelina to the rescue!" said Angelina, and she skipped down the hallway to find her sister.

"Time to brush your teeth, Polly," said Angelina, but Polly wasn't in her cozy bed. Polly wasn't anywhere in her room, and she wasn't in the bathroom either. Angelina looked in all Polly's

usual hiding places, even under the bed,
but she couldn't find Polly anywhere.

"Blueberry pancakes for breakfast!" Mrs. Mouseling called from the kitchen. Angelina loved blueberry pancakes, and she leapt down the stairs two at a time. At the bottom she stopped and listened. She could hear snuffling noises coming from the closet. Angelina opened the door and saw Polly's little pink toes peeking out.

"Why are you hiding, Polly?" asked Angelina, pushing the coats aside. "It's breakfast time, and we're having blueberry pancakes."

"I want to stay home today with Tulip," said Polly. She was sitting in the closet in her pajamas, hugging Tulip, her favorite doll.

"You're a big girl now, Polly," said Angelina. "And you're going to school, just like me. Isn't that exciting?"

"I don't want to go to school," said Polly. "I'm too shy."

Mr. Mouseling came and scooped
Polly up in his arms. "There you are!"
he said, giving her a kiss. Then he turned
to Angelina as the family sat down to
breakfast. "You were shy when you first
started school too," he reminded her.
Angelina couldn't remember feeling shy
when she was little; it
seemed such a long
time ago.

"I'm definitely not shy now," said Angelina, helping herself to pancakes.

Polly pushed her plate away. "My tummy is not hungry," she said.

"You need to eat your pancakes so you'll have energy for school," Angelina explained.

Polly shook her head. She was usually a very cheerful, friendly little mouseling, but not today. Angelina thought Polly was very cute with her soft, fluffy fur, curly tail, and adorable big brown eyes.

They loved to dress up and dance around the house together, and Polly followed her big sister everywhere, even climbing up trees. When Polly was with Angelina, she always felt strong and brave. But today Angelina was going to be away at big school, and Polly was starting preschool. Without her big sister, Polly did not feel strong or brave at all.

Chapter Two

Three Friends

As soon as breakfast was over, Angelina jumped up and found her backpack, but Polly wasn't ready—she was still in her pajamas! Angelina knew Polly needed lots of time to get dressed; she often put her clothes on backward and her shoes on the wrong feet. Luckily Angelina was there to help.

"I loved Chipping Cheddar Preschool when I was your age," she said, pulling Polly's dress over her head, "and it's right next to my big school, so I'll see you at recess."

"What if you can't find me?" Polly asked, while Angelina fixed a bow in her sister's hair.

"Don't worry. Big sisters always look out for little sisters," Angelina said kindly, and she helped Polly put on her new backpack.

"There. You look like a real schoolgirl now," she continued. "Let's go!" Angelina skipped out the door of Honeysuckle Cottage, followed by Mrs. Mouseling and Polly.

Angelina's friends Alice and Flora were waiting for her at the corner. "Here we are, Angelina!" they said, linking arms with her. "Let's walk to school together!"

The three friends twirled and danced all through the village of Chipping

Cheddar, with Polly and Mrs. Mouseling following along behind. The village looked pretty, with geraniums still blooming in cottage windows, and the crisp air smelled of autumn. Fallen leaves crackled under Angelina's feet.

"Is Polly starting preschool today?" asked Alice.

"Yes, but she's feeling shy and scared," answered Angelina.

"The first day of school isn't so easy when you're little," said Flora.

"Were you shy on your first day?" Angelina asked her friends.

Alice and Flora nodded.

"What about you?" asked Flora.

Angelina shook her head, and then she looked back. Polly was dragging her feet and clinging to her mother. "Come on, Polly!" Angelina shouted encouragement. Then the school bell started ringing, and Angelina dashed around the corner to Chipping Cheddar Elementary.

The schoolyard was filled with excited mouselings who were smiling, laughing, and greeting each other. Angelina couldn't wait to go inside the friendly red schoolhouse and meet her new teacher. She loved reading books and writing stories,

18

and she was looking forward to telling her classmates all about her summer. Angelina skipped around the schoolyard

saying hello and chatting with everyone. She was having so much fun that she forgot all about her shy little sister.

Polly and Mrs. Mouseling arrived just as the school bell started to ring.

"Angelina!" Polly shouted as loudly as she could. But Angelina was already lining up for school with her friends, and she couldn't hear Polly calling her. The school door swung open, and Angelina trotted inside. Polly hid behind her mother's skirt and peeked out at the empty schoolyard. "Where did Angelina go?" she asked.

"Don't worry, Polly, she's just gone to her classroom," said Mrs. Mouseling kindly. Polly's whiskers drooped. She really needed her big sister now, but Angelina wasn't there.

Chapter Three

Miss Whiskers and Mrs. Appleby

"Good morning! You must be Polly." A smiling teacher in a flowery dress knelt down beside Polly. "My name is Miss Whiskers, and I've come to welcome you to preschool. We have lots of fun things to do today."

Mrs. Mouseling gave Polly a hug and said, "I'll see you very soon."

Miss Whiskers took Polly by the hand and walked her into Chipping Cheddar Preschool. "Look, we're right next door to your big sister's school," said Miss Whiskers, pointing to the elementary school. Polly did not agree. To her, Angelina's school was way too far away.

★

In fact, Angelina was not far away at all. While Polly was meeting Miss Whiskers, Angelina was meeting her teacher too. After the bell rang, Angelina and her friends quickly found their classroom and filed in.

They were greeted by a teacher in a bright blue dress, who smiled and welcomed them inside. "Good morning. everyone. I'm Mrs. Appleby, and I'm delighted to see you all back at school!" she said.

Angelina liked Mrs. Appleby right away, especially her warm smile and kind voice. Angelina quickly found her desk and looked for her friends. She waved to Flora and Alice at their desks nearby.

"Good morning, Mrs. Appleby!" they all said together.

"Can anyone tell us about their favorite book they read this summer?" asked Mrs. Appleby.

Alice raised her hand. "I read all the Mindy the Mouse Detective books," she said. "I love finding out how Mindy solves all sorts of mysteries."

"What a terrific choice," said Mrs. Appleby.

"I read *The Teatime Treats Cookbook*,"
Flora told the class. "Then I made a
yummy chocolate nut cake and lots of
cheese muffins with my mom."

"How delicious!" said Mrs. Appleby.

Angelina loved reading the Mindy the Mouse Detective books, and she loved baking cakes and muffins with her mom, but she especially loved reading books about fairies and dancing. She quickly raised her hand. "I love books that make me want to dance," she said. "This summer I read *Tales of Magical Fairies* three times, and I made up lots of fairy dances with my little sister."

"How wonderful to share a love of dancing with your sister," said Mrs. Appleby.

Angelina remembered how much fun she had doing fairy dances with Polly.

She had no idea that just next door, Polly was wishing she could run away and go back home to her mother and Tulip.

"Here we are!" said Miss Whiskers, opening the door into a colorful room and leading Polly inside. Eleven little

mouselings were giggling and chatting with each other in a circle on the floor. Miss Whiskers showed Polly a cushion to sit on. "Now that we're all here, let's go around the circle and tell everyone our names," she said. One by one, the little mouselings all squeaked their names.

"I'm Johnny!" a little boy mouse squeaked.

"I'm Susie," squeaked a little girl mouse.

When it was Polly's turn, she was so scared that she could only manage the tiniest squeak. "I'm P-P-P-Polly," she stuttered.

"That was a good try, Polly," said Miss Whiskers. She turned to the little gray mouseling next to Polly. "Can you tell the class your name?" Miss Whiskers asked. But the little mouseling shook her head and stared at the floor. "This is Bella," said Miss Whiskers, patting Bella on the head.

Chapter Four

Angelina's Daydream

Around the corner at Chipping Cheddar Elementary, Angelina was as busy as a bee. In art class she helped paint a mural of autumn trees, and then she practiced handstands and cartwheels in the gym. Next it was time for history.

Mrs. Appleby pointed to a large map on the wall. "Who can tell us something about the capital of Mouseland?" she asked.

"The capital is called Great Gouda," said Flora.

Angelina stuck her hand up in the air. "That's where the Royal Dance Company is!" she added.

"Yes. And the Royal Theater too," agreed Mrs. Appleby.

Angelina had always wanted to go to the Royal Theater. She knew all about it from Miss Lilly, her dance teacher. Serena Silvertail, the most famous ballet dancer in all of Mouseland, was the prima ballerina at the Royal Theater. Angelina wished she could go there and watch Serena Silvertail perform.

While the other mouselings continued to raise their hands and answer questions, Angelina got lost in a beautiful daydream. She imagined herself doing pliés and pirouettes with the ballet dancers at the Royal Dance Company, just like Miss

Lilly. Then she imagined herself all grown up, wearing a sparkling tutu, and dancing onstage like Serena Silvertail. Ah, how wonderful to be a real ballerina dressed in a sparkling tutu, performing at the beautiful Royal Theater in Great Gouda! Angelina was so happy that she couldn't stop twirling . . . and twirling . . . and twirling. . . .

"ANGELINA! Please pay attention."
Mrs. Appleby's voice interrupted
Angelina's daydream.

"Oops, sorry," said Angelina, sitting
up straight.

Her lovely daydream faded away.

Next door at the preschool, Polly was trying to be brave and strong like her big sister. She made a finger painting with orange and red fall colors and listened to Miss Whiskers read a story about the Town Mouse and the Country Mouse. Polly usually loved anything to do with art projects and storybooks, but today she was so fidgety she could hardly sit still.

"Come sit next to Bella," said Miss Whiskers at snack time, pulling out a chair for Polly. Bella was nibbling on her cheese bar, and Polly sat next to her and nibbled on a sandwich, but they didn't say a word to each other.

Soon it was time for recess, and Bella scampered off to the playground behind the other mouselings. Polly followed them outside and watched as they ran and played together. She wished she knew how to join in their games. School was just as hard as she'd thought it would be. She didn't know how to make friends, and she was sure she would never find Angelina.

Chapter Five

A Special Surprise

At Angelina's snack time, all the mouselings shared their muffins and raisins. As soon as they finished eating, they all ran outside to the playground. Some of the other big kids were already playing tag and hopscotch, and Angelina quickly joined in, racing as fast as she could around the playground, laughing and tagging her friends. It was so much fun that she kept running until she was out of breath and had to rest. Angelina plopped down under the old oak tree, and then she heard a familiar snuffling noise. She looked all around the tree until at last she saw Polly sitting all alone.

Angelina suddenly remembered what it felt like to be small and new at school. She jumped up and gave Polly a hug. "I was shy too," she admitted, "but then I found out it's not so hard to make new friends."

"I'm too scared without you," said Polly, wiping away her tears.

"Come on, I'll show you," said Angelina, and she took Polly's hand and led her to meet the other mouselings. "This is my little sister, Polly," Angelina announced. "She loves to dance and play games, just like me."

All the big mouselings smiled and gathered around.

"Hello, Polly!" they said. "Angelina always talks about her cute little sister!"

"Hello," answered Polly, feeling a tiny bit braver.

"Do you want to play Red Light, Green Light with us?" asked Alice.

"Okay," said Polly, holding on to Angelina's hand.

"Can I play too?" asked Bella, who was standing nearby.

Polly realized Bella felt shy too, so she held out her hand, and they lined up together with Angelina and Alice. The big kids showed them lots of fun games, and

then Polly and Bella went on the swings and the slide and climbed the jungle gym together. Soon Polly and Bella were running, hopping, and jumping with all the other little mouselings on the playground. Polly didn't feel shy anymore!

Angelina watched Polly play with her new friends, and then she had a great idea. She went to talk to Miss Whiskers, who smiled and said, "Yes, that would be a lovely surprise."

At the end of the day, all the preschoolers sat in a big circle again.

"Polly's sister, Angelina, has a special treat for us today," said Miss Whiskers.

Then Angelina and her friends danced into the room.

Angelina invited all the little mouselings to join her, and then she led everyone in a twirling, swirling dance around and around the classroom.

"Welcome to Chipping Cheddar Preschool!" all the big mouselings sang. Soon everyone joined in, and even Miss Whiskers was twirling, swirling, and singing!

"What a wonderful way to celebrate our first day of school!" said Miss Whiskers. "I hope you'll come back and dance with us again."

"We will," promised Angelina and her friends.

Then it was time to go home. Polly said goodbye to Bella and Miss Whiskers. "I'll see you tomorrow!" Polly said.

"I had so much fun," she added. "I don't feel so shy anymore."

"You're a brave mouseling, Polly," said Angelina, "and I truly love you. Do you want to walk to school with me tomorrow?"

"Yes. I really truly love you too, Angelina," said Polly. "You're the best big sister ever."

Don't miss Angelina's
next adventure in *Angelina
Ballerina's Ballet Tour!*

About the Author and Illustrator

Katharine Holabird and Helen Craig are the author and illustrator of the Angelina Ballerina series, which includes more than twenty-five books. Angelina has also been adapted for television and the stage and is considered an icon in children's publishing.

Katharine Holabird is also the creator of Twinkle, a magical fairy. She lives in New York City.

In addition to Angelina Ballerina, Helen Craig has illustrated many beloved books for children. She lives in England.